THE CONQUERIN' HERO OF THE HUMBOLTS

(Politics at Blue Lizard)

BY

ROBERT E. HOWARD

British Library Cataloguing-in-Publication Data
A catalogue record for this book is available from the
British Library

Robert E. Howard

Robert Ervin Howard was born in Peaster, Texas in 1906. During his youth, his family moved between a variety of Texan boomtowns, and Howard – a bookish and somewhat introverted child – was steeped in the violent myths and legends of the Old South. Although he loved reading and learning, Howard developed a distinctly Texan, hardboiled outlook on the world. He became a passionate fan of boxing, taking it up at an amateur level, and from the age of nine began to write adventure tales of semi-historical bloodshed. In 1919, when Howard was thirteen, his family moved to the Central Texas hamlet of Cross Plains, where he would stay for the rest of his life.

At fifteen Howard began to read the pulp magazines of the day, and to write more seriously. The December 1922 issue of his high school newspaper featured two of his stories, 'Golden Hope Christmas' and 'West is West'. In 1924 he sold his first piece – a short caveman tale titled 'Spear and Fang' – for $16 to the not-yet-famous *Weird Tales* magazine. He published with the magazine regularly over the next few years. 1929 was a breakout year for Howard, in that the 23-year-old writer began to sell to other magazines, such as *Ghost Stories* and *Argosy,* both of whom had previously sent him hundreds of rejection slips. In 1930, he began a correspondence with weird fiction master H. P. Lovecraft which ran up to his death six years later, and is regarded as one of the great correspondence cycles in all of fantasy literature.

It was partly due to Lovecraft's encouragement that Howard created his most famous character, Conan the Cimmerian. Conan – a barbarian-turned-King during the Hyborian Age, a mythical period of some 12,000 years ago – featured in seventeen *Weird Tales* stories between 1933 and 1936, and is now regarded as having spawned the 'sword and sorcery' genre, making Howard's influence on fantasy literature comparable to that of J. R. R. Tolkien's. The Conan stories have since been adapted many times, most famously in the series of films starring Arnold Schwarzenegger.

Howard was enjoying an all-time high in sales by the beginning of 1936, but he was also deeply upset by the ill health of his mother, who had fallen into a coma. On the morning of June 11, 1936, he asked an attending nurse whether she would ever recover, and the nurse replied negatively. Howard walked to his car, parked outside the family home in Cross Plains, and shot himself. He died eight hours later, aged just thirty.

I was in Sundance enjoying myself a little after a long trail-drive up from the Cimarron, when I got a letter from Abednego Raxton which said as follers:

Dear Breckinridge:

That time I paid yore fine down in Tucson for breaking the county clerk's laig you said you'd gimme a hand anytime I ever need help. Well Breckinridge I need yore assistance right now the rustlers is stealing me ragged it has got so I nail my bed-kivers to the bunk every night or they'd steal the blankets right offa me Breckinridge. Moreover a stumbling block on the path of progress by the name of Ted Bissett is running sheep on the range next to me this is more'n a man can endure Breckinridge. So I want you to come up here right away and help me find out who is stealing my stock and bust Ted Bissett's hed for him the low-minded scunk. Hoping you air the same I begs to remane as usual.

Yore abused frend.

Raxton, Esq.

> P. S. That sap-headed misfit Johnny Willoughby which used to work for me down on Green River is sheriff here and he couldn't ketch flies if they was bogged down in merlasses.

Well, I didn't feel it was none of my business to mix into any row Abednego might be having with the sheepmen, so long as both sides fit fair, but rustlers was a different matter. A Elkins detests a thief. So I mounted Cap'n Kidd, after the usual battle, and headed for Lonesome Lizard, which was the nighest town to his ranch.

I found myself approaching this town a while before noon one blazing hot day, and as I crossed a right thick timbered creek, shrieks for aid and assistance suddenly bust the stillness. A hoss also neighed wildly, and Cap'n Kidd begun to snort and champ like he always does when they is a b'ar or a cougar in the vicinity. I got off and tied him, because if I was going to have to fight some critter like that, I didn't want him mixing into the scrap; he was jest as likely to kick me as the varmint. I then went on foot in the direction of the screams, which was growing more desperate every minute, and I presently come to a thicket with a big tree in the middle of it, and there they was. One of the purtiest gals I ever seen was roosting in the tree and screeching blue murder, and they was a cougar climbing up after her.

"Help!" says she wildly. "Shoot him!"

"I jest wish some of them tender-foots which calls theirselves naturalists could see this," I says, taking off my Stetson. A Elkins never forgits his manners. "Some of 'em has tried to tell me cougars never attacks human beings nor climbs trees, nor prowls in the daytime. I betcha this would make 'em realize they don't know it all. Jest like I said to that'n which I seen in War Paint, Nevada, last summer--"

"Will you stop talkin' and do somethin'?" she says fiercely. "Ow!"

Because he had reched up and made a pass at her foot
his left paw. I seen this had went far enough, so I told
nly to come down, but all he done was look down at
in a very insulting manner. So I reched up and
tail and yanked him down, and whapped
und three or four times, and when I let
a few yards, and looked back at me in
. Then he shaken his head like he
d lit a shuck as hard as he could
f the North Pole.
anded the gal, leaning as

d her. "Hey, look

me tumbling
nto the limb

with a desperate grip, however, which is why it rapped me so severe on the head when I catched her.

"Oh!" says she, letting go of the limb and grabbing me. "Am I hurt?"

"I dunno," I says, "You better let me carry you to wherever you want to go."

"No," says she, gitting her breath back. "I'm all right. Lemme down."

So I done so, and she says: "I got a hoss tied over there behind that fir. I was ridin' home from Lonesome Lizard and stopped to poke a squirrel out of a holler tree. It warn't a squirrel, though. It was that dang lion. If you'll git my hoss for me, I'll be ridin' home. Pap's ranch is jest over that ridge to the west. I'm Margaret Brewster."

"I'm Breckinridge Elkins, of Bear Creek, Nevad
I says. "I'm headin' for Lonesome Lizard, but I'll be r
back this way before long. Can I call on you?"

"Well," she says, "I'm engaged to marry a fell
it's conditional. I got a suspicion he's a spineless fai
I told him flat if he didn't succeed at the job's h
on now, not to come back. I detests a failure. T
likes yore looks," says she, giving me a admiri
man which can rassle a mountain lion with h
worth any gal's time. I'll send you word at L
if my fiansay flops like it looks he's goin' to
have you call."

"I jest wish some of them tender-foots which calls theirselves naturalists could see this," I says, taking off my Stetson. A Elkins never forgits his manners. "Some of 'em has tried to tell me cougars never attacks human beings nor climbs trees, nor prowls in the daytime. I betcha this would make 'em realize they don't know it all. Jest like I said to that'n which I seen in War Paint, Nevada, last summer--"

"Will you stop talkin' and do somethin'?" she says fiercely. "Ow!"

Because he had reched up and made a pass at her foot with his left paw. I seen this had went far enough, so I told him sternly to come down, but all he done was look down at me and spit in a very insulting manner. So I reched up and got him by the tail and yanked him down, and whapped him agen the ground three or four times, and when I let go of him he run off a few yards, and looked back at me in a most pecooliar manner. Then he shaken his head like he couldn't believe it hisself, and lit a shuck as hard as he could peel it in the general direction of the North Pole.

"Whyn't you shoot him?" demanded the gal, leaning as far out as she could to watch him.

"Aw, he won't come back," I assured her. "Hey, look out! That limb's goin' to break--"

Which it did jest as I spoke and she come tumbling down with a shriek of despair. She still held onto the limb with a desperate grip, however, which is why it rapped me so severe on the head when I catched her.

"Oh!" says she, letting go of the limb and grabbing me. "Am I hurt?"

"I dunno," I says, "You better let me carry you to wherever you want to go."

"No," says she, gitting her breath back. "I'm all right. Lemme down."

So I done so, and she says: "I got a hoss tied over there behind that fir. I was ridin' home from Lonesome Lizard and stopped to poke a squirrel out of a holler tree. It warn't a squirrel, though. It was that dang lion. If you'll git my hoss for me, I'll be ridin' home. Pap's ranch is jest over that ridge to the west. I'm Margaret Brewster."

"I'm Breckinridge Elkins, of Bear Creek, Nevada," I says. "I'm headin' for Lonesome Lizard, but I'll be ridin' back this way before long. Can I call on you?"

"Well," she says, "I'm engaged to marry a feller, but it's conditional. I got a suspicion he's a spineless failure, and I told him flat if he didn't succeed at the job's he's workin' on now, not to come back. I detests a failure. That's why I likes yore looks," says she, giving me a admiring glance. "A man which can rassle a mountain lion with his b'ar hands is worth any gal's time. I'll send you word at Lonesome Lizard; if my fiansay flops like it looks he's goin' to do, I'd admire to have you call."

"I'll be awaitin' yore message with eager heart and honest devotion," I says, and she blushed daintily and clumb on her hoss and pulled her freight. I watched her till she was clean out of sight, and then hove a sigh that shook the acorns out of the surrounding oaks, and wended my way back to Cap'n Kidd in a sort of rose-colored haze. I was so entranced I started to git onto Cap'n Kidd on the wrong end and never noticed till he kicked me vi'lently in the belly.

"Love, Cap'n Kidd," I says to him dreamily, batting him between the eyes with my pistol butt, "is youth's sweet dream."

But he made no response, outside of stomping on my corns; Cap'n Kidd has got very little sentiment.

SO I MOUNTED AND PULLED for Lonesome Lizard, which I arriv at maybe a hour later. I put Cap'n Kidd in the strongest livery stable I could find and seen he was fed and watered, and warned the stable-hands not to antagonize him, and then I headed for the Red Warrior saloon. I needed a little refreshments before I started for Abednego's ranch.

I taken me a few drams and talked to the men which was foregathered there, being mainly cowmen. The sheepmen patronized the Bucking Ram, acrost the street. That was the first time I'd ever been in Montana, and them fellers warn't familiar with my repertation, as was showed by their manner.

Howthesomever, they was perlite enough, and after we'd downed a few fingers of corn scrapings, one of 'em ast me where I was from, proving they considered me a honest man with nothing to conceal. When I told 'em, one of 'em said: "By golly, they must grow big men in Nevada, if yo're a sample. Yo're the biggest critter I ever seen in the shape of a human."

"I bet he's as stout as Big Jon," says one, and another'n says: "That cain't be. This gent is human, after all. Big Jon ain't."

I was jest fixing to ast 'em who this Jon varmint was, when one of 'em cranes his neck toward the winder and says: "Speak of the devil and you gits a whiff of brimstone! Here comes Jon acrost the street now. He must of seen this gent comin' in, and is on his way to make his usual challenge. The sight of a man as big as him is like wavin' a red flag at a bull."

I looked out the winder and seen a critter about the size of a granary coming acrost the street from the Bucking Ram, follered by a gang of men which looked like him, but not nigh as big.

"What kind of folks air they?" I ast with interest. "They ain't neither Mexicans nor Injuns, but they sure ain't white men, neither."

"Aw, they're Hunkies," says a little sawed-off cowman. "Ted Bissett brung 'em in here to herd sheep for him. That big 'un's Jon. He ain't got no sense, but you never seen sech a hunk of muscle in yore life."

"Where they from?" I ast. "Canader?"

"Naw," says he. "They come originally from a place called Yurrop. I dunno where I it is, but I jedge it's somewhere's east of Chicago."

But I knowed them fellers never originated nowheres on this continent. They was rough-dressed and wild-looking, with knives in their belts, and they didn't look like no folks I'd ever saw before. They come into the barroom and the one called Jon bristled up to me very hostile with his little beady black eyes. He stuck out his chest about a foot and hit it with his fist which was about the size of a sledge hammer. It sounded like a man beating a bass drum.

"You strong man," says he. "I strong too. We rassle, eh?"

"Naw," I says, "I don't care nothin' about rasslin'."

He give a snort which blowed the foam off of every beer glass on the bar, and looked around till he seen a iron rod laying on the floor. It looked like the handle of a branding iron, and was purty thick. He grabbed this and bent it into a V, and throwed it down on the bar in front of me, and all the other Hunkies jabbered admiringly.

This childish display irritated me, but I controlled myself and drunk another finger of whiskey, and the bartender whispered to me: "Look out for him! He aims to prod you into a fight. He's nearly kilt nine or ten men with his b'ar hands. He's a mean 'un."

"Well," I says, tossing a dollar onto the bar and turning away, "I got more important things to do than rassle a outlandish foreigner in a barroom. I got to eat my dinner and git out to the Raxton ranch quick."

But at that moment Big Jon chose to open his bazoo. There are some folks which cain't never let well enough alone.

"'Fraid!" jeered he. "Yah, yah!"

The Hunkies all whooped and guffawed, and the cattlemen scowled.

"What you mean, afraid?" I gasped, more dumbfounded than mad. It'd been so long since anybody's made a remark like that to me. I was plumb flabbergasted. Then I remembered I was amongst strangers which didn't know my repertation, and I realized it was my duty to correct that there oversight before somebody got hurt on account of ignorance.

So I said, "All right, you dumb foreign muttonhead, I'll rassle you."

But as I went up to him, he doubled up his fist and hit me severely on the nose, and them Hunkies all bust into loud, rude laughter. That warn't wise. A man had better twist a striped thunderbolt's tail than hit a Elkins onexpected on the nose. I give a roar of irritation and grabbed Big Jon and started committing mayhem on him free and enthusiastic. I swept all the glasses and bottles off of the bar with him, and knocked down a hanging lamp with him, and fanned the floor with him till he was limp, and then I throwed him the full length of the barroom. His head went through the panels of the back door, and the other Hunkies, which had stood petrified, stampeded into the street with howls of horror. So I taken the branding iron handle and straightened it out and bent it around his neck, and twisted the ends together in a knot, so he had to get a blacksmith to file it off after he come to, which was several hours later.

All them cowmen was staring at me with their eyes popped out of their heads, and seemed plumb incapable of speech, so I give a snort of disgust at the whole incerdent, and strode off to git my dinner. As I left I heard one feller, which was holding onto the bar like he was too weak to stand alone, say feebly to the dumb-founded bartender: "Gimme a drink, quick! I never thunk I'd live to see somethin' I couldn't believe when I was lookin' right smack at it."

I COULDN'T MAKE NO sense out of this, so I headed for the dining room of the Montana Hotel and Bar. But my hopes of peace and quiet was a illusion. I'd jest started on my fourth beefsteak when a big maverick in Star-top boots and store-bought clothes come surging into the dining room and bellered: "Is your name Elkins?"

"Yes, it is," I says. "But I ain't deef. You don't have to yell."

"Well, what the hell do you mean by interferin' with my business?" he squalled, ignoring my reproof.

"I dunno what yo're talkin' about," I growled, emptying the sugar bowl into my coffee cup with some irritation. It looked like Lonesome Lizard was full of maneyacks which craved destruction. "Who air you, anyhow?"

"I'm Ted Bissett, that's who!" howled he, convulsively gesturing toward his six-shooter. "And I'm onto you! You're a damn Nevada gunman old Abed' Raxton's brought up here to run me off the range! He's been braggin' about it all over town! And you starts your work by runnin' off my sheepherders!"

"What you mean, I run yore sheepherders off?" I demanded, amazed.

"They ran off after you maltreated Big Jon," he gnashed, with his face convulsed. "They're so scared of you they won't come back without double pay! You can't do this to me, you #$%&*!"

The man don't live which can call me that name with impunity. I impulsively hit him in the face with my fried steak, and he give a impassioned shriek and pulled his gun. But some grease had got in his eyes, so all he done with his first shot was bust the syrup pitcher at my elbow, and before he could cock his gun again I shot him through the arm. He dropped his gun and grabbed the place with his other hand and made some remarks which ain't fitten for to repeat.

I yelled for another steak, and Bissett yelled for a doctor, and the manager yelled for the sheriff.

The last-named individual didn't git there till after the doctor and the steak had arrove and was setting Bissett's arm--the doctor, I mean, and not the steak, which a trembling waiter brung me. Quite a crowd had gathered by this time and was watching the doctor work with great interest, and offering advice which seemed to infuriate Bissett, jedging from his langwidge. He also discussed his busted arm with considerable passion, but the doctor warn't a bit worried. You never seen sech a cheerful gent. He was jovial and gay, no matter how loud Bissett yelled. You could tell right off he was a man which could take it.

But Bissett's friends was very mad, and Jack Campbell, his foreman, was muttering something about 'em taking the law into their own hands, when the sheriff come prancing in, waving a six-shooter and hollering: "Where is he? P'int out the scoundrel to me?"

"There he is!" everybody yelled, and ducked, like they expected gunplay, but I'd already recognized the sheriff, and when he seen me he recoiled and shoved his gun out of sight like it was red hot or something.

"Breckinridge Elkins!" says he. Then he stopped and studied a while, and then he told 'em to take Bissett out to the bar and pour some licker down him. When they'd went he sot down at the table, and says: "Breck, I want you to understand that they ain't nothin' personal about this, but I got to arrest you. It's agen the law to shoot a man inside of the city limits."

"I ain't got time to git arrested," I told him. "I got to git over to old Abed' Raxton's ranch."

"But lissen, Breck," argyed the sheriff--it was Johnny Willoughby, jest like old Abed' said--"what'll folks think if I don't jail you for shootin' a leadin' citizen? Election's comin' up and my hat's in the ring," says he, gulping my coffee.

"Bissett shot at me first," I said. "Whyn't you arrest him?"

"Well, he didn't hit you," says Johnny, absently cramming half a pie into his mouth and making a stab at my pertaters. "Anyway, he's got a busted arm and ain't able to go to jail jest now. Besides, I needs the sheepmen's votes."

"Aw, I don't like jails," I said irritably, and he begun to weep.

"If you was a friend to me," sobs he, "you'd be glad to spend a night in jail to help me git re-elected. I'd do as much for you! The whole county's givin' me hell anyway, because I ain't been able to catch none of them cattle rustlers, and if I don't arrest you I won't have a Chinaman's chance at the polls. How can you do me like this, after the times we had together in the old days--"

"Aw, stop blubberin'," I says. "You can arrest me, if you want to. What's the fine?"

"I don't want to collect no fine, Breck," says he, wiping his eyes on the oil-cloth table cover and filling his pockets with doughnuts. "I figgers a jail sentence will give me more prestige. I'll let you out first thing in the mornin'. You won't tear up the jail, will you, Breck?"

I promised I wouldn't, and then he wants me to give up my guns, and I refuses.

"But good gosh, Breck," he pleaded. "It'd look awful funny for a prisoner to keep on his shootin' irons."

So I give 'em to him, jest to shet him up, and then he wanted to put his handcuffs onto me, but they warn't big enough to fit my wrists. So he said if I'd lend him some money he could have the blacksmith to make me some laig-irons, but I refused profanely, so he said all right, it was jest a suggestion, and no offense intended, so we went down to the jail. The jailer was off sleeping off a drunk somewheres, but he'd left the key hanging on the door, so we went in. Purty soon along come Johnny's deperty, Bige Gantry, a long, loose-j'inted cuss with a dangerous eye, so Johnny sent him to the Red Warrior for a can of beer, and whilst he was gone Johnny bragged on him a heap.

"Why," says he, "Bige is the only man in the county which has ever got within' shootin' distance of them dern outlaws. He was by hisself, wuss luck. If I'd been along we'd of scuppered the whole gang."

I ast him if he had any idee who they was, and he said Bige believed they was a gang up from Wyoming. So I said well, then, in that case they got a hang-out in the hills somewheres, and ought to be easier to run down than men which scattered to their homes after each raid.

BIGE GOT BACK WITH THE beer about then, and Johnny told him that when I got out of jail he was going to depertize me and we'd all go after them outlaws together. So Bige said that was great, and looked me over purty sharp, and we sot down and started playing poker. Along about supper time the jailer come in, looking tolerable seedy, and Johnny made him cook us some supper. Whilst we was eating the jailer stuck his head into my cell and said: "A gent is out there cravin' audience with Mister Elkins."

"Tell him the prisoner's busy," says Johnny.

"I done so," says the jailer, "and he says if you don't let him in purty dern quick, he's goin' to bust in and cut yore throat."

"That must be old Abed' Raxton," says Johnny. "Better let him in--Breck," says he, "I looks to you to pertect me if the old cuss gits mean."

So old Abed' come walzing into the jail with fire in his eye and corn licker on his breath. At the sight of me he let out a squall which was painful to hear.

"A hell of a help you be, you big lummox!" he hollered. "I sends for you to help me bust up a gang of rustlers and sheepherders, and the first thing you does is to git in jail!"

"T'warn't my fault," I says. "Them sheepherders started pickin' on me."

"Well," he snarls, "whyn't you drill Bissett center when you was at it?"

"I come up here to shoot rustlers, not sheepherders," I says.

"What's the difference?" he snarled.

"Them sheepmen has probably got as much right on the range as you cowmen," I says.

"Cease sech outrageous blasphermy," says he, shocked. "You've bungled things so far, but they's one good thing--Bissett had to hire back his derned Hunkie herders at double wages. He don't no more mind spendin' money than he does spillin' his own blood, the cussed tightwad. Well, what's yore fine?"

"Ain't no fine," I said. "Johnny wants me to stay in jail a while."

At this old Abed' convulsively went for his gun and Johnny got behind me and hollered: "Don't you dast shoot a ossifer of the law!"

"It's a spite trick!" gibbered old Abed'. "He's been mad at me ever since I fired him off'n my payroll. After I kicked him off'n my ranch he run for sheriff, and the night of the election everybody was so drunk they voted for him by mistake, or for a joke, or somethin', and since he's been in office he's been lettin' the sheepmen steal me right out of house and home."

"That's a lie," says Johnny heatedly. "I've give you as much pertection as anybody else, you old buzzard! I jest ain't been able to run any of them critters down, that's all. But you wait! Bige is on their trail, and we'll have 'em behind the bars before the snow falls."

"Before the snow falls in Guatemala, maybe," snorted old Abed'. "All right, blast you, I'm goin', but I'll have Breckinridge outa here if I have to burn the cussed jail! A Raxton never forgits!" So he stalked out sulphurously, only turning back to snort: "Sheriff! Bah! Seven murders in the county unsolved since you come into office! You'll let the sheepmen murder us all in our beds! We ain't had a hangin' since you was elected!"

After he'd left, Johnny brooded a while, and finally says: "The old lobo's right about them murders, only he neglected to mention that four of 'em was sheepmen. I know it's cattlemen and sheepmen killin' each other, each side accusin' the other'n of rustlin' stock, but I cain't prove nothin'. A hangin' would set me solid with the voters." Here he eyed me hungrily, and ventured: "If somebody'd jest up and confess to some of them murders--"

"You needn't to look at me like that," I says. "I never kilt nobody in Montana."

"Well," he argyed, "nobody could prove you never done 'em, and after you was hanged--"

"Lissen here, you," I says with some passion, "I'm willin' to help a friend git elected all I can, but they's a limit!"

"Oh, well, all right," he sighed. "I didn't much figger you'd be willin', anyway; folks is so dern selfish these days. All they thinks about is theirselves. But lissen here: if I was to bust up a lynchin' mob it'd be nigh as good a boost for my campaign as a legal hangin'. I tell you what--tonight I'll have some of my friends put on masks and come and take you out and pretend like they was goin' to hang you. Then when they got the rope around yore neck I'll run out and shoot in the air and they'll run off and I'll git credit for upholdin' law and order. Folks always disapproves of mobs, unless they happens to be in 'em."

So I said all right, and he urged me to be careful and not hurt none of 'em, because they was all his friends and would be mine. I ast him would they bust the door down, and he said they warn't no use in damaging property like that; they could hold up the jailer and take the key off'n him. So he went off to fix things, and after while Bige Gantry left and said he was on the trace of a clue to them cattle rustlers, and the jailer started drinking hair tonic mixed with tequila, and in about a hour he was stiffer'n a wet lariat.

WELL, I LAID DOWN ON the floor on a blanket to sleep, without taking my boots off, and about midnight a gang of men in masks come and they didn't have to hold up the jailer, because he was out cold. So they taken the key off'n him, and all the loose change and plug tobaccer out of his pockets too, and opened the door, and I ast: "Air you the gents which is goin' to hang me?" And they says: "We be!"

So I got up and ast them if they had any licker, and one of 'em gimme a good snort out of his hip flask, and I said: "All right, le's git it over with, so I can go back to sleep."

He was the only one which done any talking, and the rest didn't say a word. I figgered they was bashful. He said: "Le's tie yore hands behind you so's to make it look real," and I said all right, and they tied me with some rawhide thongs which I reckon would of held the average man all right.

So I went outside with 'em, and they was a oak tree right clost to the jail nigh some bushes. I figgered Johnny was hiding over behind them bushes.

They had a barrel for me to stand on, and I got onto it, and they throwed a rope over a big limb and put the noose around my neck, and the feller says: "Any last words?"

"Aw, hell," I says, "this is plumb silly. Ain't it about time for Johnny--"

At this moment they kicked the barrel out from under me.

Well, I was kind of surprized, but I tensed my neck muscles, and waited for Johnny to rush out and rescue me, but he didn't come, and the noose began to pinch the back of my neck, so I got disgusted and says: "Hey, lemme down!"

Then one of 'em which hadn't spoke before says: "By golly, I never heard a man talk after he'd been strung up before!"

I recognized that voice; it was Jack Campbell, Bissett's foreman! Well, I have got a quick mind, in spite of what my cousin Bearfield Buckner says, so I knowed right off something was fishy about this business. So I snapped the thongs on my wrists and reched up and caught hold of the rope I was hung with by both hands and broke it. Them scoundrels was so surprized they didn't think to shoot at me till the rope was already broke, and then the bullets all went over me as I fell. When they started shooting I knowed they meant me no good, and acted according.

I dropped right in the midst of 'em, and brung three to the ground with me, and during the few seconds to taken me to choke and batter them unconscious the others was scairt to fire for fear of hitting their friends, we was so tangled up. So they clustered around and started beating me over the head with their gun butts, and I riz up like a b'ar amongst a pack of hounds and grabbed four more of 'em and hugged 'em till their ribs cracked. Their masks came off during the process, revealing the faces of Bissett's friends; I'd saw 'em in the hotel.

Somebody prodded me in the hind laig with a bowie at that moment, which infuriated me, so I throwed them four amongst the crowd and hit out right and left, knocking over a man or so at each lick, till I seen a wagon spoke on the ground and stooped over to pick it up. When I done that somebody throwed a coat over my head and blinded me, and six or seven men then jumped onto my back. About this time I stumbled over some feller which had been knocked down, and fell onto my belly, and they all started jumping up and down on me enthusiastically. I reched around and grabbed one and dragged him around to where I could rech his left ear with my teeth. I would of taken it clean off at the first snap, only I had to bite through the coat which was over my head, but as it was I done a good job, jedging from his awful shrieks.

He put forth a supreme effort and tore away, taking the coat with him, and I shaken off the others and riz up in spite of their puny efforts, with the wagon spoke in my hand.

A wagon spoke is a good, comforting implement to have in a melee, and very demoralizing to the enemy. This'n busted all to pieces about the fourth or fifth lick, but that was enough. Them which was able to run had all took to their heels, leaving the battlefield strewed with moaning and cussing figgers.

Their remarks was shocking to hear, but I give 'em no heed. I headed for the sheriff's office, mad clean through. It was a few hundred yards east of the jail, and jest as I rounded the jail house, I run smack into a dim figger which come sneaking through the bresh making a curious clanking noise. It hit me with what appeared to be a iron bar, so I went to the ground with it and choked it and beat its head agen the ground, till the moon come out from behind a cloud and revealed the bewhiskered features of old Abednego Raxton!

"What the hell?" I demanded of the universe at large. "Is everybody in Montaner crazy? Whar air you doin' tryin' to murder me in my sleep?"

"I warn't, you jack-eared lunkhead," snarled he, when he could talk.

"Then what'd you hit me with that there pinch bar for?" I demanded.

"I didn't know it was you," says he, gitting up and dusting his britches. "I thought it was a grizzly b'ar when you riz up out of the dark. Did you bust out?"

"Naw, I never," I said. "I told you I was stayin' in jail to do Johnny a favor. And you know what that son of Baliol done? He framed it up with Bissett's friends to git me hung. Come on. I'm goin' over and interview the dern skunk right now."

So we went over to Johnny's office, and the door was unlocked and a candle burning, but he warn't in sight.

* * *

THEY WAS A SMALL IRON safe there, which I figgered he had my guns locked up in, so I got a rock and busted it open, and sure enough there my shooting-irons was. They was also a gallon of corn licker there, and me and Abed' was discussing whether or not we had the moral right to drink it, when I heard somebody remark in a muffled voice: "Whumpff! Gfuph! Oompg!"

So we looked around and I seen a pair of spurs sticking out from under a camp cot over in the corner. I grabbed hold of the boots they was on, and pulled 'em out, and a human figger come with 'em. It was Johnny. He was tied hand and foot and gagged, and he had a lump onto his head about the size of a turkey aig.

I pulled off the gag, and the first thing he says was: "If you sons of Perdition drinks my private licker I'll have yore hearts' blood!"

"You better do some explainin'," I says resentfully. "What you mean, siccin' Bissett's friends onto me?"

"I never done no sech!" says he heatedly. "Right after I left the jail I come to the office here, and was jest fixin' to git hold of my friends to frame the fake necktie party, when somebody come in at the door and hit me over the head. I thought it was Bige comin' in and didn't look around, and then whoever it was clouted me. I jest while ago come to myself, and I was tied up like you see."

"If he's tellin' the truth," says old Abed' "--which he seems to be, much as I hates to admit it--it looks like some friend of Bissett's overheard you all talkin' about this thing, follered Johnny over and put him out of the way for the time bein', and then raised a mob of his own, knowin' Breck wouldn't put up no resistance, thinkin' they was friends. I told you--who's that?"

We all drawed our irons, and then put 'em up as Bige Gantry rushed in, holding onto the side of his head, which was all bloody.

"I jest had a bresh with the outlaws!" he hollered. "I been trailin' 'em all night! They waylaid me while ago, three miles out of town! They nearly shot my ear off! But if I didn't wing one of 'em, I'm a Dutchman!"

"Round up a posse!" howled Johnny, grabbing a Winchester and cartridge belt. "Take us back to where you had the scrape, Bige--"

"Wait a minute," I says, grabbing Bige. "Lemme see that ear!" I jerked his hand away, disregarding the spur he stuck into my laig, and bellered: "Shot, hell! That ear was chawed, and I'm the man which done it! You was one of them illegitimates which tried to hang me!"

He then whipped out his gun, but I knocked it out of his hand and hit him on the jaw and knocked him through the door. I then follered him outside and taken away the bowie he drawed as he rose groggily, and throwed him back into the office, and went in and throwed him out again, and went out and throwed him back in again.

"How long is this goin' on?" he ast.

"Probably all night," I assured him. "The way I feel right now I can keep heavin' you in and out of this office from now till noon tomorrer."

"Hold up!" gurgled he. "I'm a hard nut, but I know when I'm licked! I'll confess! I done it!"

"Done what?" I demanded.

"I hit Johnny on the head and tied him up!" he howled, grabbing wildly for the door jamb as he went past it. "I rigged the lynchin' party! I'm in with the rustlers!"

"Set him down!" hollered Abed', grabbing holt of my shirt. "Quick, Johnny! Help me hold Breckinridge before he kills a valurebull witness!"

But I shaken him off impatiently and sot Gantry onto his feet. He couldn't stand, so I helt him up by the collar and he gasped: "I lied about tradin' shots with the outlaws. I been foolin' Johnny all along. The rustlers ain't no Wyoming gang; they all live around here. Ted Bissett is the head chief of 'em--"

"Ted Bissett, hey?" whooped Abed', doing a war-dance and kicking my shins in his glee. "See there, you big lummox? What'd I tell you? What you think now, after showin' so dern much affection for them cussed sheepmen? Jest shootin' Bissett in the arm, like he was yore brother, or somethin'! S'wonder you didn't invite him out to dinner. You ain't got the--"

"Aw, shet up!" I said fretfully. "Go on, Gantry."

"He ain't a legitimate sheepman," says he. "That's jest a blind, him runnin' sheep. Ain't no real sheepmen mixed up with him. His gang is jest the scrapin's of the country, and they hide out on his ranch when things gits hot. Other times they scatters and goes home. They're the ones which has been killin' honest sheepman and cattlemen--tryin' to set the different factions agen each other, so as to make stealin' easier. The Hunkies ain't in on the deal. He jest brung 'em out to herd his sheep, because his own men wouldn't do it, and he was afeared if he hired local sheepherders, they'd ketch onto him. Naturally we wanted you outa the way, when we knowed you'd come up here to run down the rustlers, so tonight I seen my chance when Johnny started talkin' about stagin' that fake hangin'. I follered Johnny and tapped him on the head and tied him up and went and told Bissett about the business, and we got the boys together, and you know the rest. It was a peach of a frame-up, and it'd of worked, too, if we'd been dealing with a human bein'. Lock me up. All I want right now is a good, quiet penitentiary where I'll be safe."

"Well," I said to Johnny, after he'd locked Gantry up, "all you got to do is ride over to Bissett's ranch and arrest him. He's laid up with his arm, and most of his men is crippled. You'll find a number of 'em over by the jail. This oughta elect you."

"It will!" says he, doing a war-dance in his glee. "I'm as good as elected right now! And I tell you, Breck, t'ain't the job alone I'm thinkin' about. I'd of lost my gal if I'd lost the race. But she's promised to marry me if I ketched them rustlers and got re-elected. And she won't go back on her word, neither!"

"Yeah?" I says with idle interest, thinking of my own true love. "What's her name?"

"Margaret Brewster!" says he.

"What?" I yelled, in a voice which knocked old Abed' over on his back like he'd been hit by a cyclone. Them which accuses me of vi'lent and onusual conduck don't consider how my emotions was stirred up by the knowledge that I had went through all them humiliating experiences jest to help a rival take my gal away from me. Throwing Johnny through the office winder and kicking the walls out of the building was jest a mild expression of the way I felt about the whole dern affair, and instead of feeling resentful, he ought to have been thankful I was able to restrain my natural feelings as well as I done.

www.ingramcontent.com/pod-product-compliance
Lightning Source LLC
LaVergne TN
LVHW041929090826
845145LV00017B/2779